Cleo in the Snow

Stella Blackstone
Caroline Mockford

Barefoot Books
Step inside a story

Cleo wakes. Cleo winks.

Cleo yawns. Cleo blinks.

Cleo goes outside.
Cleo stops to stare.

The garden is all
white and cold,
with snowflakes
everywhere.

Cleo sniffs.
Cleo swipes.

Caspar sniffs.
Caspar bites.

"Come and sit with me!"

Caspar
swiftly
slides
downhill.

Cleo watches warily.

Cleo has a ride.

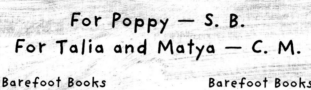

For Poppy — S. B.
For Talia and Matya — C. M.

Barefoot Books
2067 Massachusetts Ave
Cambridge, MA 02140

Barefoot Books
294 Banbury Road
Oxford, OX2 7ED

Graphic design by Jennie Hoare, England, and Louise Millar, England
Reproduction by B & P International, Hong Kong
Printed in China on 100% acid-free paper
This book was set in Carrotflower and Providence Sans Bold
The illustrations were prepared in acrylics

Board book ISBN: 978-1-78285-054-0
Paperback ISBN: 978-1-78285-055-7

British Cataloguing-in-Publication Data:
a catalogue record for this book
is available from the British Library

1 3 5 7 9 8 6 4 2